CLEMATIS &
CLIMBERS

LANCE HATTATT

Illustrations by
ELAINE FRANKS

This edition first published in 1997 by
Parragon
Units 13–17 Avonbridge Trading Estate
Atlantic Road, Avonmouth
Bristol BS11 9QD

Produced by
Robert Ditchfield Publishers

ISBN 0 75252 138 1

A copy of the British Library Cataloguing in Publication
Data is available from the Library.

Typeset by Action Typesetting Ltd, Gloucester
Colour origination by Colour Quest Graphic Services Ltd,
London E9
Printed and bound in Italy

"With thanks to **J**"

SYMBOLS

Where measurements are given, the first is the plant's height
followed by its spread.
The following symbols are also used in this book:
  ○ = thrives best or only in full sun
  ◑ = thrives best or only in part-shade
  ● = succeeds in full shade
  E = evergreen
Where no sun symbol and no reference to sun or shade is
made in the text, it can be assumed that the plant tolerates
sun or light shade.

POISONOUS PLANTS

Many plants are poisonous and it must be assumed that no
part of a plant should be eaten unless it is known that it is
edible.

CONTENTS

CLEMATIS AND CLIMBERS

Clematis and climbers are the soft furnishings of the garden. They contribute a luxuriant, well-appointed effect, adding both height and interest. Additionally, where used to climb through trees and shrubs they extend the season of the host plant. The introduction of climbers into a small garden, where space is restricted and therefore at a premium, greatly increases the range of plants to be grown.

WHICH CLIMBER?

Whatever the situation, however difficult, a climber is available to meet all but the most impossible of requirements. Evergreen ivies, many with bright, variegated foliage, will often flourish in dry, shady conditions where the soil is poor and thin. The shelter of a wall, perhaps that of the house, will allow many less hardy subjects to be grown with considerable success. Against a much frequented path the fragrance of a scented honeysuckle may be enjoyed to the full. For interest over an extended period the small-flowered clematis which later carry fluffy seedheads are an excellent choice. A conservatory or glasshouse where a constant temperature is maintained during colder months will allow all manner of tender climbers to be grown.

SUITABLE SITES

Correct growing conditions will ensure healthy, successful plants. Before planting it is advisable to introduce and work in generous quantities of well rotted manure or garden compost. During dry periods plants should be kept well watered until they

Opposite: *Clematis* 'Fireworks' grows over a wooden quadripod.

Clematis and honeysuckle intertwine to great effect.

are fully established. When positioning a climber against a wall, ascertain that any roof overhang does not preclude rain reaching the roots. Clematis, particularly, are rich feeders and will welcome an annual top dressing of organic matter.

Some climbers are self-supporting, ivies for example; others will require tying-in. A cane positioned at the base of the plant and directed towards the host will encourage shoots in the desired direction. Such supports should be put in place at the time of planting to avoid damage to the plant's root system. All ties should be checked regularly and not allowed to cut into stems. Smooth surfaces can be faced with plastic-coated mesh, chicken wire or studded with fastenings to assist young tendrils.

Many climbers are unfussy about situation. Others

Rosa 'Zéphirine Drouhin' is planted to make a screen.

will require certain conditions to be satisfied. It may be the protection of a warm wall, safeguarding new shoots against slugs or, as in the case of clematis, shading roots from the sun. For this a large stone placed at the base of the plant should be adequate. Planting instructions should be heeded.

CARING FOR CLIMBERS

Once established many climbers will require little attention beyond checking ties, eliminating dead wood, the thinning of overcrowded branches and an annual feed. Indeed, pruning should not be regarded as a potential problem but rather as a matter of common sense. More often than not it is sufficient simply to maintain a healthy framework, taking out spindly or diseased stems. As a general rule of thumb, little harm will result from pruning immediately after flowering.

Clematis are often regarded as a special case. Contrary to popular belief, pruning techniques are not at all complicated. Early-flowering clematis require little pruning beyond the removal of weak and dead stems once flowering is over. Large-flowered hybrids, blooming before midsummer, should be lightly pruned, which involves removing tangled growth and generally thinning-out after flowering. Those flowering later, on the current season's stems, should be cut back hard to ground level during the winter months. New, young shoots will shortly appear.

COMPANION PLANTINGS

Climbers should be used in profusion, with generosity of spirit. Team them with trees, with shrubs and with each other. Use as ground cover or as a focal point in pots and containers. Have them cascading down and scaling heights. Planted in these ways the most wonderful and original effects can be realized. Planting schemes are limitless; with a little experimentation the most exciting combinations can be achieved.

There can be no hard and fast rules. White flowers look startlingly brilliant against the dark green of a clipped yew hedge. Red flowers, such as those of the scarlet *Tropaeolum speciosum*, in the same situation make a very different, but equally powerful, kind of statement. Pale pinks in semi-shade gleam with a luminosity, dark pinks in full sun demand to be noticed. Purple on gold is distinctive, purple mixed with grey is moody and Gothic. Imagination and a sense of purpose are the only requirements to transform the garden into something exceptional and very beautiful.

Opposite: *Tropaeolum speciosum* (Flame flower) glows against a yew hedge.

1. CLEMATIS

AN EARLY SHOW

TINY NODDING HEADS of the delightful alpina and macropetala clematis are amongst the first to appear. Grown through shrubs, which will flower later in the year, or to scramble into evergreen trees, they add an extra and welcome dimension.

This Ali Baba jar would make an excellent subject for a patio or any sitting-out area. Here the pretty pink heads of *Clematis alpina* **'Ruby'** and the blue *C. alpina* **'Frances Rivis'** jostle over the edges.

Clematis alpina will grow very happily in a cool, shady situation and be amongst the first to flower.

***Clematis macropetala* 'Maidwell Hall'** Violet blue flowers contrast with the lime green bracts of *Euphorbia amygdaloides robbiae*.

Clematis armandii Evergreen clematis, very vigorous, early and long-flowering (see also PLANTS WITH PERFUME)

***Clematis macropetala* 'Blue Bird'** Fresh foliage complements the clear blue of this early spring flower.

Clematis cirrhosa An evergreen producing welcome blooms in late winter.

CLIMBING HEIGHTS

No ultimate heights are given for clematis. These will depend on area, aspect, situation and soil type. Nearly all can be controlled and contained with regular pruning.

Most clematis will tolerate sun or shade, though their roots must always be shaded. Some flowers fade less if they are out of the sun.

PRUNING THE MONTANAS

Flowering during the early spring, *Clematis montana* and its various forms need little in the way of pruning. Established plants should have dead or weak stems removed after the flowering period. Flowers form on new shoots, so if you prune later you will remove the following year's display.

Clematis montana This most attractive clematis remains understandably popular. It looks especially good in the evening light.

Clematis chrysocoma makes a very acceptable alternative to the more vigorous montanas where space is restricted. A profusion of soft pink flowers are displayed against downy foliage which is slightly bronze tinted.

BOLD *and* BEAUTIFUL

FOR DRAMA AND IMPACT these must be the first choice. Main flowering season is given though the blooms are often recurrent.

Clematis 'Ville de Lyon'
This clematis is a popular choice as it is scarcely without flower during the summer months.

◆ *For early blooms, prune lightly. To restrict growth to around 3m/10ft, hard prune.*

Here the deep wine red of *Clematis* **'Madame Edouard André'** associates with the clear blue of the ever popular *Clematis* **'Perle d'Azur'**.

***Clematis* 'Barbara Dibley'** A moderate grower with flowers of deep red fading, as here, to pale magenta. Early summer.

***Clematis* 'Barbara Jackman'** Superb colour, elegant shape and vigorous, healthy growth in this marvellous plant. Early summer.

***Clematis* 'Marie Boisselot'** Absolutely lovely for its sheer whiteness once the large flowers have fully opened. Midsummer.

◆ *'Marie Boisselot' is sometimes sold as 'Madame le Coultre'. The two plants are identical.*

***Clematis* 'Duchess of Sutherland'** Carmine-red blooms are produced on the current season's growth. Midsummer.

***Clematis* 'Miss Bateman'** The purple leaves of the cotinus are a perfect foil to the attractive flower heads. Early summer.

***Clematis* 'Comtesse de Bouchaud'** Pearly mauve-pink flowers which shine through the foliage of host trees or shrubs. Late summer.

◆ *This vigorous clematis is deservedly popular with its masses of blooms.*

***Clematis* 'Nelly Moser'** One of the best known and loved of all clematis and a prolific flowerer. Early summer.

***Clematis* 'Ernest Markham'** is amongst the strongest growers of the large-flowered hybrids. Late summer.

***Clematis* 'Maureen'** A comparatively modern clematis introduced during the 1950s. For best results, prune lightly. Midsummer.

***Clematis* 'Lord Nevill'** One of the most intensely blue of all clematis with a second flowering in autumn. Early summer.

***Clematis* 'W.E. Gladstone'** Exceedingly large flowers of up to 25cm/10in. Midsummer.

Always shade the roots of clematis with a stone slab, thick mulch or another plant. Plant 10cm/4in deeper than in the container as insurance against wilt.

Clematis **'Arctic Queen'** is seen here fully clothing a wooden pyramid with a mass of unusual double flowers. Early summer.

◆ *A simple wooden pyramid is the best way to train clematis in a pot.*

CHOICE CLEMATIS

TO GIVE THE GARDEN SOMETHING SPECIAL, seek out those clematis which are less often cultivated.

Clematis rehderiana An absolute delight when the delicate, fragrant flowers are arranged to fall at eye level. Late.

Clematis recta is an herbaceous perennial growing up to 2m/6ft in a season. It may require some support. Midsummer.

Clematis florida 'Alba Plena' Surely one of the most desirable of all clematis for its lovely greenish-white blooms. Late.

◆ *Afford this clematis the protection of a warm wall or grow as a conservatory plant.*

***Clematis* × *eriostemon* 'Hendersonii'** An excellent subject to encourage as light ground cover through the border. Late.

Clematis* × *aromatica The lemony scent of this rather charming little flower is somewhat evasive but worth pursuing.

***Clematis florida* 'Sieboldii'** Often mistaken for a passion flower, the joy of this appealing clematis is the deep purple centre set against creamy sepals. Position in a sunny spot or, alternatively, grow as a container specimen. Late.

LATE-FLOWERING TEXENSIS HYBRIDS are delightful climbers to incorporate into the garden scene.

Clematis texensis '**Etoile Rose**' Possibly the loveliest of all the texensis varieties, though seldom seen.

◆ *Texensis clematis require hard pruning early in the year.*

Clematis* × *durandii
Somewhat reluctant to climb, *durandii* is at its best given the support of a twiggy shrub. Midsummer.

Clematis forsteri Afford some shelter to this wonderfully fragrant, early flowering, evergreen clematis.

***Clematis* 'Royalty'** Rich purple tones befit this aptly named hybrid. Early.

***Clematis* 'Dr. Ruppel'** A good, strong grower which flowers freely throughout the summer.

***Clematis* 'Lady Londesborough'** As the flowers tend to come together, this is a plant for a showy situation. Early.

LATE PERFORMERS

As the blooms of many of the large-flowered hybrids go over, so they are replaced with clematis which will provide a point of interest for late summer into autumn.

A delightful combination is achieved in this garden scene by placing together the two late flowerers *Clematis* **'Huldine'** and *Clematis viticella* **'Royal Velours'**.

Clematis tangutica This yellow flowered species is well known, well liked and widely grown.

Clematis 'Lasurstern' Although less prolific than earlier in the season, 'Lasurstern' will flower reliably at the year's end.

Clematis 'Viticella Rubra' Formerly named 'Kermesina' this variety has bright crimson flowers.

Clematis viticella 'Madame Julia Correvon' A beautiful deep red shade to bring colour towards the close of season.

These lingering seedheads have a quiet charm long after the flowers are forgotten.

Clematis viticella '**Margot Koster**' Very floriferous with brilliant, narrow magenta sepals.

CLEMATIS WILT

The main symptom of wilt is the sudden collapse of an otherwise healthy plant. Treatment should include the removal to the ground of all diseased material, the application of a sulphur-based fungicide, a mulch of fresh compost and copious watering.

Always plant the root-ball of clematis up to 10cm/4in deeper than the soil-level in the container to enable it to throw up new shoots from below the level of the soil, if it has been affected by the disease.

Clematis viticella **'Purpurea Plena Elegans'** A double flower which, because of its smallness, is especially appealing.

Clematis × jouiniana **'Praecox'** A non-clinging clematis which should be allowed to roam at will.

Clematis viticella **'Etoile Violette'** will, when established, flower to the point of almost obscuring the foliage.

2. CLIMBING
ROSES

PASTEL SHADES

CLIMBING ROSES are not demanding plants to grow. Give them a fertilizer when planting, repeat as necessary and mulch in spring to conserve moisture.

***Rosa* 'Paul's Himalayan Musk'** Dainty sprays of blush blooms in midsummer. 9m/30ft

◆ *This is a strong grower and can cover a tree.*

Rosa **'Madame Grégoire Staechelin'** Plant this against a sunless wall and experience these wonderful, early, fleshy blooms. 6m/20ft

Rosa **'Souvenir de la Malmaison Climber'** This beautiful blush rose flowers twice, the second crop being the better. 3.5m/12ft

Rosa **'Paul's Lemon Pillar'** Strong growth, huge lemony white flowers and fine perfume. 6m/20ft

Rosa 'Albertine' Deservedly popular, this splendid near double rose is heavily fragrant. 5.5m/18ft

◆ *Train 'Albertine' against a wall or permit it to scramble among shrubs.*

Rosa 'Albéric Barbier' Soft yellow flowers later become creamy white. It is rarely without some flower. 6m/20ft

HOT *and* SMOKY

A blaze of colour is
achieved when the
double orange-scarlet blooms
of *Rosa* **'Danse du Feu'**
intermingle with the deep yellow
of *Clematis tangutica*. The bronze
tinted foliage of this spirited
modern climbing rose adds lustre.

ICE COOL

CREAM AND WHITE ROSES suggest
flowery bowers. As a centrepiece to an
all-white garden, to climb into old
fruit trees or to garland ropes, the
choice is immense.

Rosa **'Iceberg'** The
climbing form of this
floribunda carries masses of
pure white flowers over
shining leaves. 3m/10ft

Rosa **'Sanders' White'**
deserves a place in every
garden where its true
beauty can readily be
appreciated. 2.4m/8ft

Rosa **'Félicité et Perpétue'**
is a classic rose whose
double rosette flowers are a
constant source of pleasure.
3.5m/12ft

Rosa **'Rambling Rector'**
This is a rose to grow
through old trees where
vigour can be left
unchecked. 10m/33ft

Care should be taken when considering *Rosa filipes* **'Kiftsgate'**. This extraordinary rose has enormous growth potential and is only suitable where space really is unlimited.

3. CLIMBERS

ALL-YEAR INTEREST

VARIEGATED LEAVES, patterned foliage,
simple, unassuming flowers and even
twisted branches are but a few of the
reasons why some climbers are valued
throughout the year. These are plants
which perform an important,
supporting rôle.

Wisterias remain one of the most popular and, indeed, one
of the most charming of all climbers. In addition to
attractive, fresh green foliage and beautiful flower racemes,
mature plants are noted for their interesting, gnarled wood.

Chaenomeles × superba **'Rowallane'** These pretty flowers will continue well after the leaves are fully out. 1m/3ft

Jasminum nudiflorum remains attractive even when leafless in winter. Winter jasmine is ideal for training. 2.4m/8ft

Chaenomeles speciosa **'Nivalis'** (Japonica, flowering quince) White flowers on bare stems will later be followed by traditional quinces. 2m/6ft

Actinidia kolomikta has unusual leaves which, grown in full sun, are splashed pink and white. 3.5m/12ft

***Hedera helix* 'Goldheart'** is a small-leafed ivy with enormous vigour but apt to revert to green. E, 2.7m/9ft

***Hedera colchica* 'Sulphur Heart'** Brilliant variegation on large leaves lightens up the gloomiest corner. E, 4.5m/15ft

Polygonum baldschuanicum The Russian vine, or mile-a-minute, will smother any structure in a short while. ○, 12m/39ft

Hydrangea anomala petiolaris This climbing hydrangea will thrive on a sunless wall. Self-clinging. 8m/26ft

AUTUMN TINTS

BRIGHT BERRIES and burnished leaves conjure up the sights, sounds and smells of autumn. Virginia creepers lit by a dying sun, purple-leafed vines and spent golden hops are all late players.

Hollies are especially appealing at this time of the year, their glossy berries warming up drab days. Here *Ilex aquifolium* '**J C van Tol**' has almost spineless leaves with abundant red berries.

Vitis coignetiae The crimson glory vine is trained in this instance around a pillar. 15m/49ft

Parthenocissus tricuspidata **'Veitchii'** The Boston ivy will in time cover a large area, supporting itself with self-clinging tendrils. 20m/66ft

Pyracantha in its many forms will produce a mass of bright berries in autumn. E, 2.1m/7ft

◆ *Around this cottage the trained pyracantha has formed part of the architecture.*

CLIMBERS *with* STYLE

SOME GARDEN SITUATIONS demand special treatment. It may be that a dominant mood or theme requires extending. These climbers, used with imagination and thought, will do just that.

Lonicera × tellmanniana
Although lacking scent this honeysuckle has really bold orange-yellow flowers.
◐ 5m/16ft

Lathyrus latifolius 'White Pearl' An excellent white form of the everlasting pea to include in almost any planting. ○, 2m/6ft

Ipomoea 'Early Call'
(Morning glory) A splendid and exotic-looking half-hardy climber to flower for the entire summer. ○, 3m/10ft

Convolvulus althaeoides
Well suited to scramble over
low walls. Pretty but tender
and needs frost protection.
○, 1m/3ft

Wattakaka sinensis This is a
climber to add interest to
an arch or pergola. Plant in
sun. E, 2.7m/9ft

Tropaeolum speciosum makes a magnificent show of scarlet
when grown against a dark background. 2m/6ft

◆ *Occasionally the flowers are followed by deep blue berries from
which new plants can be grown.*

***Fremontodendron*
'California Glory'** Brilliant
yellow blooms continue
throughout the summer on
this quick-growing wall
shrub. O, E, 6m/20ft

***Cestrum elegans* 'Smithii'**
Inclined to be tender so in
need of wall protection. O,
E, 3m/10ft

Fremontodendron mexicanum Flowers appear a little more
starry than those of 'California Glory'. O, E, 6m/20ft

◆ *This is one of the longest blooming wall shrubs that can be
grown – from late spring to mid-autumn.*

***Solanum jasminoides* 'Album'** An exceedingly lovely climber. This form, 'Album', is probably without equal. ○, semi-E, 6m/20ft

Passiflora caerulea The well-known passion flower is a vigorous grower. Small orange fruits follow the exquisite blooms. ○, 6m/20ft

Ribes speciosum The fuchsia-flowered currant is at its best against a light background as shown here. ○, 2.4m/8ft

◆ *Dark shiny foliage, rich red, sophisticated fuchsia-like flowers and a graceful form make this a shrub difficult to surpass.*

PLANTS *with* PERFUME

SURROUND a sitting-out area with fragrant climbers trained up house walls, up posts or specially constructed pyramids.

Lathyrus odoratus
'Catherine' Surely every garden should play host to the original sweet peas. ○, 2m/6ft

Clematis armandii A most welcome sight in the early spring, not least for the powerful scent. E, ○, 4.5m/15ft

Given sufficient space the common jasmine, *Jasminum officinale*, will delight with its clusters of trumpet flowers. Here it is combined with the enticingly fragrant *Rosa* '**Ena Harkness**'.

***Lonicera periclymenum*
'Serotina'** Purplish-
crimson flowers, the
insides of which are
cream, carry an enticing
perfume. 7m/23ft

◆ *Most honeysuckles
enjoy full sun or semi-
shade and are unfussy
about soil conditions.*

Lonicera etrusca Long, branching flower panicles clothe an old brick wall in creamy yellow touched with red. Not hardy. ○, 4m/13ft

Lonicera japonica **'Halliana'** Fast growing with evergreen foliage and perfumed flowers in summer. E, 4m/13ft

Wisteria floribunda **'Multijuga'** is noted for its long racemes which are beautiful when left to hang free. ○, 9m/30ft

Cytisus battandieri Smelling of pineapple, the Moroccan broom is an outstanding shrub to train against a wall. ○, semi-E, 4m/13ft

Akebia quinata An interesting, free-growing climber, exceedingly fragrant, but requiring the shelter of a wall. ○, 9m/30ft

BERRIES *and* FRUIT

FRUITS, EDIBLE OR OTHERWISE,
produced by some climbers add a
further dimension to an attractive and
interesting plant.

Actinidia chinensis, the Chinese gooseberry, produces these
handsome kiwi fruits in a warm area where both sexes are
grown together. A companion planting of **Schisandra
rubriflora** is in fruit with a berry not dissimilar to a large
redcurrant.

A plant of *Actinidia chinensis* will grow to around 6m/20ft.
Schizandra rubriflora at around 2.7m/9ft would make an
elegant covering for an archway.

SHRUBS *as* CLIMBERS

MANY GARDEN-WORTHY SHRUBS will
respond well to being given a different
treatment and trained to grow against
a wall or fence. Some, indeed, will
benefit and produce bigger flowers
over a longer period.

Ceanothus 'Trewithen Blue'
Best grown against a wall
where the intense blue
flowers will be displayed to
effect. E, 2m/6ft

Pittosporum All forms of
this attractive, evergreen
shrub benefit from the
protection of a wall or
fence. E, 2.4m/8ft

Philadelphus 'Belle Etoile'
This form of the mock
orange, trained here against
a wall, is a mass of fragrant
flowers in midsummer. ○,
2.4m/8ft

**Leptospermum scoparium
'Alfred Coates'** This New
Zealand tea tree flowers late
spring to summer. E, 3m/10ft

***Escallonia* 'Iveyi'** Compact shrub with large racemes of scented white flowers mid- to late summer. E, 3m/10ft

Buddleja davidii will be perfectly happy tied into a wall or fence to produce a spectacular floral display. ○, 2.4m/8ft

Lavatera maritima bicolor
Tree mallows give both height and interest in the border. 1.5m/5ft

◆ *Take cuttings in case it dies in winter.*

Mahonia aquifolium is a deservedly popular evergreen, seen here carrying clusters of deep purple berries. E, 2m/6ft

***Abelia* 'Edward Goucher'** Wall protection suits this sun-loving shrub. Dark pink flowers make for a late show. 2m/6ft

Chimonanthus praecox Winter sweet is, as its name suggests, wonderfully scented and lovely when cut for indoors. 2.4m/8ft

***Euonymus fortunei* 'Silver Queen'** has exceedingly attractive variegated foliage becoming creamier as the year progresses. E, 2.4m/8ft

Itea ilicifolia should be trained against a warm wall. E, 2.7m/9ft

◆ *These fragrant racemes appear mid- to late summer.*

Magnolia grandiflora **'Exmouth'** will in time make a splendid wall shrub. Large, scented flowers are an added bonus. ◯, E, 9m/30ft

Camellia **'Waterlily'** Given acid soil camellias will perform well. ◑, E, 2m/6ft

Hydrangea quercifolia The oak-loafed hydrangea has beautiful leaves and flowers midsummer to autumn. 2m/6ft

Cotoneaster horizontalis naturally grows in a fan-like shape and is covered in berries throughout the autumn. 2m/6ft

Abutilon vitifolium 'Album'
This white form has flowers not unlike those of a hollyhock. ○, 2.4m/8ft

Phygelius capensis has unusually but effectively here been trained against a sunny wall. ○, 2.4m/8ft

Abutilon megapotamicum Well worth growing for an abundance of conspicuous red and yellow flowers. E, 2.4m/8ft

◆ *To succeed this shrub requires the warmth of a wall in full sun.*

Feijoa sellowiana Totally exotic in every way. The Pineapple guava sometimes produces edible fruits later in the year. ○, E, 2.4m/8ft

Robinia kelseyi is not always easy to train as the branches are inclined to break easily. ○, 2.4m/8ft

Callistemon rigidus These 'bottle brushes' are an absolute delight and are carried above lemon-scented foliage. E, 3m/10ft

◆ *Callistemon must be grown in well drained, acid soil in a sunny position.*

ALL *in a* YEAR

IN COLD AREAS, liable to frosts, a number of perennial climbers may be grown as annuals. With some protection, many of these climbers may prove to be hardier than was previously thought.

Rhodochiton atrosanguineus A most intriguing and utterly striking climber from Mexico with strange red and purple flowers. ○, 3m/10ft

◆ *Following the flowers, interest is maintained with balloon-like seed capsules.*

Tropaeolum tuberosum A striking climber which, as its name suggests, arises from an underground tuber. ○, 1.5m/5ft

Eccremocarpus scaber Popularly known as the Chilean glory vine, it is noted for its orange and yellow flowers. ○, 4m/13ft

Eccremocarpus scaber coccineus A red form with typical tubular flowers. Easily raised from seed. ○, 4m/13ft

Jasminum polyanthum is deliciously scented and will thrive in a cool conservatory. Keep away from direct heat. E, 2.7m/9ft+

Plumbago capensis is happiest when left to scramble amongst other plantings. Hard prune in spring. ○, 4m/13ft

***Solanum crispum* 'Glasnevin'** Rich purple flowers single out this particular form. Frost-hardy to –5°C/23°F. ○, E or semi-E, 6m/20ft

Index of Plants